TESSA KRAILING

The Petsitters Club

6. Trixie and the Cyber Pet

Illustrated by Jan Lewis

First edition for the United States, Canada, and the Philippines published by Barron's Educational Series, Inc., 1998.

First published in Great Britain in 1997 by Scholastic Children's Books, Commonwealth House, 1-19 New Oxford Street, London WC1A 1NU, UK
A division of Scholastic Ltd

All inquiries should be addressed to:

Barron's Educational Series, Inc.
250 Wireless Boulevard
Hauppauge, New York 11788
http://www.barronseduc.com

ISBN 0-7641-0614-7
Library of Congress Catalog Card No. 97-38855

Library of Congress Cataloging-in-Publication Data

Krailing, Tessa, 1935-
The Petsitters Club. 6, Trixie and the cyber pet / Tessa Krailing.—1st ed.
p. cm.
Summary: The members of the Petsitters Club find themselves very busy when they agree to take care of a pampered Yorkshire Terrier and the "virtual pup" of a classmate who has to have his tonsils out.
ISBN 0-7641-0614-7
[1. Clubs—Fiction. 2. Dogs—Fiction.] I. Title.
PZ7.K85855Pei 1998
[Fic]—dc21 97-38855
CIP
AC

Printed in the United States of America
9 8 7 6 5

Piece of Cake

The telephone rang. Sam picked it up. "Hello?" she said.

"Hello, is this the petsitting service?" asked a rather important-sounding female voice.

"Yes, it is," said Sam. "Did you want . . . ?"

"My name is Mrs. Potter-Bunn," said the voice. "I've just read your ad on the grocery store bulletin board. It says you take care of any pets, large or small, and that you are the experts. Is this true?"

"Well, we're *sort* of experts," said Sam. "Matthew and I do a lot of dog walking. And Matthew's sister Katie has creepy-crawlies. And Jo's father is a vet, so between us. . . ."

"Next Tuesday my husband and I have to go out of town for three days," said Mrs. Potter-Bunn. "And I need someone to watch my dog. Where do you live?"

Sam told her the address. "But I'm afraid we don't. . . ."

"We will come over at two-thirty to inspect the premises," said Mrs. Potter-Bunn. "Goodbye."

Sam put down the telephone. What a bossy woman! And what did she mean by "inspect the premises"?

"Sam?" Dad called from his den, where he was working on his comic strip. "Who was that on the phone?"

"Someone called Mrs. Potter-Bunn," she told him. "She's going out of town for three days and wants the Petsitters to watch her dog. It's a good thing it's semester break."

"Didn't you tell her that you don't run a boarding kennel?"

"I tried, but she kept interrupting," said Sam. "She's coming over this afternoon to 'inspect the premises.' I'd better get Matthew to come, too. After all, he's supposed to be the dog expert."

By two-thirty, all four Petsitters were in Sam's kitchen, waiting for Mrs. Potter-Bunn to arrive.

"Did she say what kind of a dog?" asked Matthew.

Sam shook her head.

"I bet it's a guard dog," said Jovan

gloomily. "Something big and fierce that only eats raw meat."

"If it was a guard dog, she'd leave it at home in case they get robbed," said Matthew.

Katie yawned. "Dogs are boring, anyway. I'm going home to play with my cockroach." She stood up.

At that moment the doorbell rang.

"That's her," said Sam.

All four Petsitters crowded into the hall. Sam opened the door.

A large, commanding woman stood on the doorstep, clutching a pocketbook.

Behind her lurked a small man with a bald head and a nervous, twitchy mustache. There was no sign of a dog.

"I am Mrs. Potter-Bunn," announced the woman. "And this is Trixie."

Sam blinked. Trixie seemed an odd name for a man.

Then she saw a small face poking out of Mrs. Potter-Bunn's pocketbook. It had perky ears, bright button eyes, and a red bow on top of its head.

"Oh!" said Sam. "It's a Yorkshire Terrier."

"Ruff!" barked Trixie.

"Yorkshire terror is more like it," muttered the man. His wife turned and gave him a withering glare.

"Please come in," said Sam.

They stepped inside. Sam closed the door.

"By the way, this is my husband," said Mrs. Potter-Bunn, waving a hand at the twitchy man.

"I'm Sam," said Sam. "And this is Matthew, Jovan, and Katie."

Mrs. Potter-Bunn cast a critical eye over the other Petsitters. "You look rather young to be experts. Trixie is very precious to me. I need to be sure she's in safe hands."

"Well, actually," said Sam, "we don't usually watch dogs for more than a few hours. Couldn't you put her in a boarding kennel?"

Mrs. Potter-Bunn shuddered. "Last time we went away I left her in a boarding kennel. Would you believe, they tried to feed her ordinary dog food? Trixie has a very delicate stomach. She's used to nothing but the best."

"Er, what kind of food *does* she eat?" Sam asked nervously.

"Don't worry, I will supply everything she needs. Is this the living room?" Mrs. Potter-Bunn marched through the open door, followed by the Petsitters and—last of all—her husband.

Sam immediately wished she had straightened up. The room was messy, but that was partly Dad's fault. He had a habit of leaving half-finished cartoons all over the place.

"Now, my precious," Mrs. Potter-Bunn said to her dog, "I'm going to let you inspect the premises yourself. After all, you're the one who will have to stay here. Have a good look around and tell me what you think."

She took Trixie out of her pocketbook and put her on the carpet.

"She's very small," said Jovan, sounding relieved.

"I've never seen such a tiny little dog," said Matthew.

"I don't usually like dogs much," said Katie, "but she's sweet."

Trixie set off at a trot to inspect the room. She disappeared behind the couch and came out with fluff on her nose.

She climbed into the wastepaper basket and climbed out again. She explored under the table and sniffed at the bookshelves. Finally she jumped up on the armchair and settled down with her head on her paws.

"She likes it!" exclaimed Mrs. Potter-Bunn. "By the way, how much do you charge?"

"We don't charge anything," said Sam. "It's part of our school's community service program. We just ask you to sign a form to say you're satisfied, that's all."

"Excellent. I will bring her over next Tuesday afternoon."

She scooped Trixie up in her arms and marched from the room, followed by her twitchy husband. Sam went to the front door to see them out.

When she came back, she said, "Well, it looks like we're stuck with taking care of Trixie. Still, she's very small. I don't think she'll be much trouble."

"Piece of cake, I bet," said Matthew.

Martin Bagshaw

“We have a new petsitting job,” Jovan told his father, Dr. Roy the veterinarian, at breakfast on Tuesday.

“Mmm,” said Dr. Roy from behind the newspaper.

“Watching someone’s dog,” Jovan explained. “It’s for three whole days, so we’re going to take turns. It wouldn’t be fair to leave it all to Sam.”

On his way to Sam's that afternoon, Jovan heard someone call his name. He turned to see Martin Bagshaw running after him, very red in the face.

"I just—stopped at—your house," panted Martin. "Your mom told me—where you were going. I was afraid I'd—missed you."

"You nearly did," said Jovan. "Did you want something? Only, I'm in a bit of a hurry."

Martin gulped. He was small for his age and had brown hair that stuck up in tufts. "I'm going into the hospital tomorrow," he said. "I have to have my tonsils out."

"Oh, too bad," said Jovan. "Still, you probably won't be in there long."

"Two days." Martin's chin began to wobble.

"Don't be scared," said Jovan. "I had

"Mmm," said Dr. Roy.

"Luckily it's only a small dog. Her name's Trixie."

Dr. Roy dropped the newspaper. He stared at Jovan. "Did you say Trixie?"

"Yes, she's a Yorkshire Terrier. I can't remember her owner's name. It's a funny name. . . ."

"Mrs. Potter-Bunn?"

"That's right," said Jovan. "And her husband has a twitchy mustache. Do you know them?"

"Oh, yes," Dr. Roy said grimly. "I know Mrs. Potter-Bunn all right. She visits my office at least once a week. Feeds her poor dog all the wrong food, then wants to know why it's always getting sick."

Jovan nodded. "She told us Trixie has a delicate stomach."

"Delicate stomach my foot! I keep telling her, all that dog needs is a sensible diet. But she won't listen." Dr. Roy folded up his newspaper and rose from the table. "And you're going to watch Trixie while she's away?"

"Yes. Well, Sam is, mainly. But as I said, we're going to take turns."

"Then I wish you good luck," said Dr. Roy. "I bet you'll need it!"

mine out last year. It doesn't hurt much and the nurses are really nice."

Martin gulped. "Trouble is, Mom says I can't take Henry with me. That's why I came to see you. Could the Petsitters look after him while I'm in the hospital?"

"I'm afraid we're a bit busy right now," said Jovan. "We have to watch somebody's dog for three days . . ."

Martin's mouth turned down at the corners.

". . . but I think we can manage both," said Jovan quickly. "What kind of an animal is Henry?"

"He's not exactly an animal." Martin fished in his pocket and brought out a small pink object with yellow buttons and a screen. "He's my cyber pet."

"A *cyber* pet!" Jovan wanted to laugh. "Oh, I think we can watch that okay. Give it to me."

Reluctantly Martin handed over his pet. "He needs a lot of attention. You have to press these buttons to keep him fed, otherwise he loses weight. And if he's unhappy, he beeps. That's why Mom says I can't take him to the hospital, in case he disturbs other people."

"Don't worry." Jovan slipped the cyber pet into his pocket. "Henry will be safe with us."

Martin wiped his eyes with the back of his hand. "Thanks, Jo."

"No problem," said Jovan.

Grinning to himself, he hurried on to Sam's house.

Trixie Arrives

"Where's Jo?" Sam asked, when Matthew and Katie arrived.

"He's coming," said Katie. "We saw him talking to Martin Bagshaw."

"Who's Martin Bagshaw?" asked Sam.

"You know," said Matthew. "He's that funny little kid with tufty hair like someone out of a cartoon."

"You mean he looks like this?" Sam's dad drew a cartoon character on his drawing pad.

"Pretty much," said Matthew.

The doorbell rang. Everyone jumped.

"I bet that's the Potter-Bunns," said Sam.

She opened the front door. Mrs. Potter-Bunn stood on the step with Trixie in her arms. Behind her lurked Mr. Potter-Bunn, laden with luggage.

"Here we are!" Mrs. Potter-Bunn marched into the hall without waiting to be asked. "Where should we put Trixie's luggage? I warn you, there's a lot of it."

"More than we're taking on our trip," muttered Mr. Potter-Bunn.

"Er, in the living room, please," said Sam.

Mrs. Potter-Bunn sailed into the living room, followed by her husband.

"Put those bags down, Gerald, and get the rest from the car." She turned to Sam. "These are her toys. She's very fond of them, especially the mouse. She loves her little mousey, don't you, my precious?"

"Ruff!" barked Trixie.

Matthew and Katie appeared in the doorway, with Sam's dad close behind them. They watched, fascinated, as Mr. Potter-Bunn brought in more bags and put them down. Finally he carried in Trixie's dog bed, beautifully upholstered in red velvet. By the time he had finished, he looked hot and twitchy.

In the middle of this excitement, Jovan arrived.

"Sorry I'm late," he said. "But I got caught by Martin Bagshaw. You'll never guess what. . . ." He stopped, staring at the pile of bags on the living room floor. "Wow, what's all this?"

"Trixie's luggage," said Sam.

"The food should go straight into the

refrigerator," said Mrs. Potter-Bunn. "It's in separate containers, marked clearly for each day we will be away. She's already had her main meal for today. She won't need anything else until about six, when she has a snack of bread and cheese."

"Best cheddar," muttered Mr. Potter-Bunn. "*I* only get the cheap stuff."

His wife gave him a frosty look. "We

will come to get her on Friday at dinner time. Oh, and if you're worried about her health, take her straight to Dr. Roy the vet."

"That's Jo's dad," said Sam, pointing at Jovan.

Mrs. Potter-Bunn turned to the dog in her arms. "Did you hear that, my precious? This is your friend Dr. Roy's son. He's going to watch you while we're away."

"Ruff!" barked Trixie.

Mrs. Potter-Bunn got misty-eyed. "Oh dear, I hate leaving her. We have to leave because our son's getting married. . . ."

"Hand her over quick," growled her husband, "and let's get going."

"Goodbye, my precious." Mrs. Potter-Bunn kissed Trixie's topknot. She stared into her bright button eyes. "It's only until Friday. And I will bring you back a present, I promise. A big piece of wedding cake."

"Ruff!" barked Trixie.

"If you don't get a move on, we'll miss that train." Mr. Potter-Bunn was already heading for the door.

Mrs. Potter-Bunn choked back a sob. She thrust Trixie into Sam's arms and hurried after her husband.

"What about walks?" Matthew called out. "Did you give us her leash?"

Mrs. Potter-Bunn shook her head. "She's too delicate to go out for walks. I'm afraid she might pick up nasty germs." Head bowed, she got into the car beside her husband and they drove off.

Matthew closed the door and returned to the others. "Boy, who ever heard of a dog who's too delicate to go out for walks!"

Sam noticed her father sneaking off. "Dad? Dad, you're not going to put the Potter-Bunns in a comic strip, are you?"

But he had already gone into the den and closed the door.

Sam sighed. "Poor Trixie," she murmured, stroking the little dog's head. "Don't be sad. We'll take care of you."

"It's lucky Jo's dad is their vet," said Matthew.

Jovan looked thoughtful. "When I told him we'd be watching Trixie, he wished us good luck. He thinks we're going to need it."

"That's silly," said Katie. "She's a sweet little thing. Can I hold her, Sam?"

"If you want." Sam handed Trixie over carefully. "I'd better start unpacking her luggage."

"Ruff!" barked Trixie and licked Katie's ear.

Yuck!

Sam carried the bags containing Trixie's food into the kitchen and started unpacking. The contents of each foil dish was marked clearly in black ink:

Matthew and Jovan came into the kitchen.

"Wow!" said Matthew when he saw the labels. "No wonder Mrs. Potter-Bunn said Trixie was used to nothing but the best."

"This is human food," said Jovan. "It's too rich for a dog."

"Just what I was thinking," Sam opened the refrigerator door and started putting in the foil containers.

"My dad says Mrs. Potter-Bunn comes to his office about once a week," said Jovan. "He keeps telling her to put Trixie on a sensible diet, but she won't listen."

At that moment Katie appeared in the doorway with a disgusted look on her face. "Trixie just got sick!" she said. "All over your living room carpet, Sam."

Sam groaned. "I'd better clean it up before Dad sees it."

She grabbed a piece of paper towel, a cloth, and some stain remover and went into the living room. The others followed. Trixie, still looking sorry for herself, sat and watched while Sam mopped up the mess.

Jovan said, "Seems like my dad was right about the food. Mrs. Potter-Bunn said Trixie had already had her main meal for today. I bet it was something rich."

"Spaghetti and meat sauce, by the look of it," said Matthew, peering over his shoulder.

"YUCK!" said Katie.

"Ruff!" said Trixie. But it was a sad, apologetic little bark.

"Don't worry, Trixie." Sam patted her on the head. "We're not angry with you. You couldn't help being sick."

BEEP, BEEP, BEEP, BEEP!

"What was that?" Sam looked around the room.

"What was what?" asked Katie, who was busy playing with a spider she had found scuttling across the floor.

"I thought I heard a beeping noise," said Sam.

"Must have been Trixie," said Matthew.

"Trixie doesn't go beep, beep. She goes 'Ruff, ruff'!" said Sam.

"Ruff! Ruff!" barked Trixie.

BEEP, BEEP, BEEP, BEEP!

Matthew sat up. "What *is* that?"

BEEP, BEEP, BEEP, BEEP!

They all turned to stare at Jovan. "It's you!" said Sam. "You're making the noise."

"No, I'm not. Oh, wait a minute." Jovan fumbled in his pocket and brought out a small pink object. "I forgot about this."

BEEP, BEEP, BEEP, BEEP!

The others crowded around. "What is it?" asked Katie.

"Martin Bagshaw's cyber pet," said Jovan. "That's why I was late. He asked me if we could watch it while he's in the hospital for two days. It's called Henry."

Sam peered at the screen, where an odd-looking creature kept walking from side to side. "What's it supposed to be?" she asked.

"A dog, I think," said Jovan. "Although it doesn't look much like one."

BEEP, BEEP, BEEP, BEEP!

"Why does it keep making that noise?" asked Matthew.

"I guess it wants something." Jovan peered closely at the screen. "The question is, what?"

BEEP, BEEP, BEEP, BEEP!

"Didn't Martin give you any instructions?" asked Matthew.

"No, he didn't. He just said I had to

keep Henry fed and happy." Jovan tried pressing the buttons. Some little signs came up on the screen.

"That one means food," said Katie. "I know, because a boy in my class has a cyber pet."

Jovan pressed the button again. The cyber pet played a little tune.

"That means it's happy," said Katie.

"Ruff! Ruff!" Trixie pawed at Jovan's knee.

"She wants to see the cyber pet," said Sam. "Show it to her, Jo."

Jovan showed Trixie the cyber pet. Trixie sniffed at it curiously, then tried to take it in her mouth.

"I think she wants to play with it," said Katie.

"Or eat it," said Matthew. "I bet she's feeling hungry after throwing up all her dinner on the carpet. Her stomach must be empty."

"Too bad." Jovan removed Henry from Trixie's jaws and put him safely back in his pocket. "Martin Bagshaw will never forgive me if I let his cyber pet get eaten up."

"Ruff!" barked Trixie, jumping up at Jovan's pocket.

"If she *is* hungry," said Sam slowly, "I'm not going to give her any of that rich cheese for her evening snack. I'll get some dog biscuits, the special kind for small dogs, and give her those instead."

"Good idea," agreed Jovan.

Tons of Energy

The next morning Matthew and Katie came over to Sam's house.

"How's Trixie?" asked Katie.

"Fine, thanks." Sam yawned. "But I'm worn out. She cried last night so I let her come on my bed. And then she snored like an express train! I hardly slept at all."

"Ruff! Ruff!" barked Trixie.

"I borrowed a leash," said Matthew. "Me and Katie will take her out for a walk if you like."

Sam looked doubtful. "Mrs. Potter-Bunn said she was too delicate to go out for walks."

"I don't believe that. Look at the way she's bouncing around. I bet she has tons of energy." He clipped the leash onto Trixie's collar. "Come on, Trixie. Walkies!"

"Ruff! Ruff!" She whirled around in excited circles.

"Oh, wait," said Sam. "I haven't put her ribbon on yet. She needs it to keep the hair out of her eyes, otherwise she won't be able to see where she's going."

At last Trixie was ready to go out. She dragged Katie and Matthew down the hall with surprising strength for such a small dog. The front door slammed behind them.

Sam sank into the nearest chair. The house seemed blissfully quiet. Dad was working in his den. Nothing stirred. Nothing *barked*. She closed her eyes.

The doorbell rang. Sam woke with a jolt. She rubbed the sleep from her eyes and went to answer it.

"Hello, Sam." Jovan walked past her into the hall, carrying a paper bag. "I had an awful night. Henry is very demanding. If you don't look after him right he beeps like crazy. I'm worn out."

"Huh!" said Sam. "You should try looking after Trixie."

Jovan put down the bag and took the cyber pet out of his pocket. He stared down at the screen. "You have to keep feeding him or he loses weight. This morning he went down to 4 pounds. I was worried."

"Jo," said Sam. "It's not *alive*. It's only a *thing*."

But Jovan wasn't listening. "If you don't play games with him he gets bored. And at breakfast he made a poop."

"What, a real one?"

"No, of course not a real one. But I felt pretty embarrassed all the same." He looked around the room. "Where's Trixie?"

"Matthew and Katie took her out for a walk."

"I wish I'd gotten here earlier," he said. "They could have taken Henry, too, and given me a rest."

"Ruff! Ruff!" barked a voice from outside.

"Sounds like they're back." Sam got up from the chair and went to open the door.

Trixie shot past her into the hall.

Matthew and Katie followed, red-faced and weary. "Whew!" said Matthew, collapsing into a chair. "You can tell she doesn't get taken out for walks very often. She got so excited when we reached the park."

"She's not afraid of anything," said Katie. "She growled at a Rottweiler and he was *terrified*."

"She tried to chase a cat," said Matthew. "And wasn't at all upset when it spat at her."

"She's really brave for such a little dog," said Katie.

Sam grinned. "No wonder Mr. Potter-Bunn called her the Yorkshire terror!"

BEEP, BEEP, BEEP, BEEP!

Jovan groaned. "There he goes again. I wonder what he wants this time." He stared down at Henry's face.

BEEP, BEEP, BEEP, BEEP!

"He *can't* want something to eat," said Jovan. "I just fed him. Honestly, he's like a little child, always wanting attention."

BEEP, BEEP, BEEP, BEEP!

"Oh, shut up!" Jovan threw the cyber pet onto the couch in disgust.

"Don't be so mean." Katie knelt down and began to stroke it. "Poor Henry. Poor little cyber pet."

"Ruff! Ruff!" Trixie jumped onto the couch. She nuzzled the cyber pet and took it gently between her teeth.

Matthew grinned. "She really likes Henry. I think she likes him better than her little mousey."

Jovan shrugged. "She can have him for all I care."

BEEP, BEEP, BEEP, BEEP! went the cyber pet.

"Ruff, ruff," went Trixie.

"What's that smell?" Matthew sniffed the air.

Sam sniffed, too. "Oh, no!" she exclaimed.

She raced into the kitchen, followed by the others. Dad sat at the table, knife and fork in hand.

"Dad, what are you eating?"

"Lamb with dumplings," he said. "I found it in the refrigerator. It had Wednesday written on the lid, so I put it in a dish and stuck it in the oven. Don't worry, I left enough for you."

She took out the casserole dish and looked inside. “Dad, this is Trixie’s dinner, not ours! We’re having cold ham and salad.”

Dad made a face. “I’d rather have lamb.”

Sam sighed. “Oh well, I bet she’d only have thrown it up again anyway. I wish we had some good dog food to give her.”

"Oh! I nearly forgot." Jovan dashed out of the kitchen.

"Forgot what?" The others stared at each other.

Jovan came back holding the bag he had brought with him. "When I told Dad what happened yesterday he said we had a really good opportunity to put her on a good diet, even if it's only for

three days. And he gave me this." He opened the bag and showed them a supply of dog food.

Sam peered at it doubtfully. "I don't think Trixie will eat that. Mrs. Potter-Bunn said she was used to nothing but the best."

"It's worth a try, though," said Matthew. "Let's give it to her."

They looked for Trixie.

But Trixie was nowhere to be seen.

Neither was the cyber pet.

Hunt for the Cyber Pet

They hunted all over the house. At last they found Trixie curled up in her bed, sleeping peacefully. She had a happy little smile on her face.

"I bet she ate it," said Katie. "That's what she did. I bet you anything she ate Martin Bagshaw's cyber pet!"

"She couldn't have," said Sam. "Her mouth's too small for her to swallow it whole. And she couldn't have chewed it up, or there'd be pieces everywhere."

"Well, it's disappeared," said Matthew. "So where is it?"

Jovan felt terrible. Martin Bagshaw had asked him to watch his cyber pet and now he had lost it. If only he hadn't thrown it down in disgust and said that Trixie could have it for all he cared, this disaster would never have happened.

Sam picked up the little dog from her cushion. She pressed her ear to Trixie's stomach.

"What are you doing?" asked Jovan.

"Listening for the beep. If she *did* swallow the cyber pet, we should be able to hear it." She listened again, then shook her head. "Not a sound."

She put Trixie back in her basket. Trixie wagged her tail and put her head to one side, as if to say, *Look how good I am! How could you possibly suspect me of eating a cyber pet?*

"Well, if she didn't eat it, I bet she hid it," said Katie.

"Okay, let's play hunt for the cyber pet," said Sam.

They hunted upstairs and downstairs, under beds, under cushions, under the couch, and under the chairs. They looked in every corner, turned over wastepaper baskets, searched everywhere that could possibly be a hiding place.

Trixie joined in, sniffing their heels and licking their faces. She seemed to think it was some kind of game.

Then Matthew said, “I’ve just noticed. She has mud on her nose.”

They stared at Trixie. She stared back, wagging her tail a little uncertainly. Sure enough, her small black nose was smudged with traces of mud.

"She *is* a terrier, after all," said Matthew. "Terriers like to dig holes. And they bury things."

"But she hasn't been in the garden," said Jovan. "Has she?"

"She *could* have been," said Sam slowly. "Did anyone notice if the back door was open when we were talking to Dad?"

Jovan tried to think back. He pictured

himself standing in the kitchen . . . and Sam's father sitting at the table, reading the newspaper . . . and behind him . . . ?

He shook his head. "It's no good. I can't remember."

"Let's go and ask him," said Matthew.

They raced back to the kitchen, followed by Trixie. Sam's father was still eating, and behind him, the back door stood open!

"Dad, when did you open the back door?" asked Sam. "Was it before you started cooking the lamb?"

Her father looked up in surprise. "Yes, I felt I needed some fresh air. Why do you . . . ?"

Before he could finish, the Petsitters had raced into the garden, with Trixie close behind them. "Now *where?*" said Sam. "Where did you hide it, Trixie?"

Trixie wagged her tail. She looked up at them with her head to one side as if she didn't *quite* understand the question.

"Look for some fresh dirt," said Matthew. "Somewhere that's been recently dug."

They started to hunt, and again Trixie joined in the game.

"The trouble is," said Sam, "that if she buried it, we won't be able to hear the beep. It's too faint."

"And if it stays buried too long, it'll stop beeping altogether," said Matthew.

Jovan felt close to despair. Henry was lost forever. And it was all his fault!

Suddenly Sam said, "Look at Trixie!"

The other Petsitters turned to see the little dog busily digging a hole in the vegetable garden. She was digging like crazy with her front paws, sending clumps of earth flying out behind her. They hurried over to take a closer look.

"What's she doing?" asked Sam. "Do you think she's digging up the cyber pet?"

"She might be," said Matthew cautiously. "After all, that's what terriers do. They bury things and then they dig them up again."

Jovan moved Trixie gently out of the way. He knelt down and put his ear close to the hole.

"Can you hear anything?" asked Sam.

"I think so," said Jovan. "I'm not sure."

He listened again. Yes, there it was, a faint, hiccuping be-ep, be-ep, be-ep coming from just below the surface.

He began to burrow in the earth with his hands. Within seconds his fingers touched something round and hard. He pulled it out and stared at it. It was the cyber pet all right, a dirty, neglected, sad-looking cyber pet.

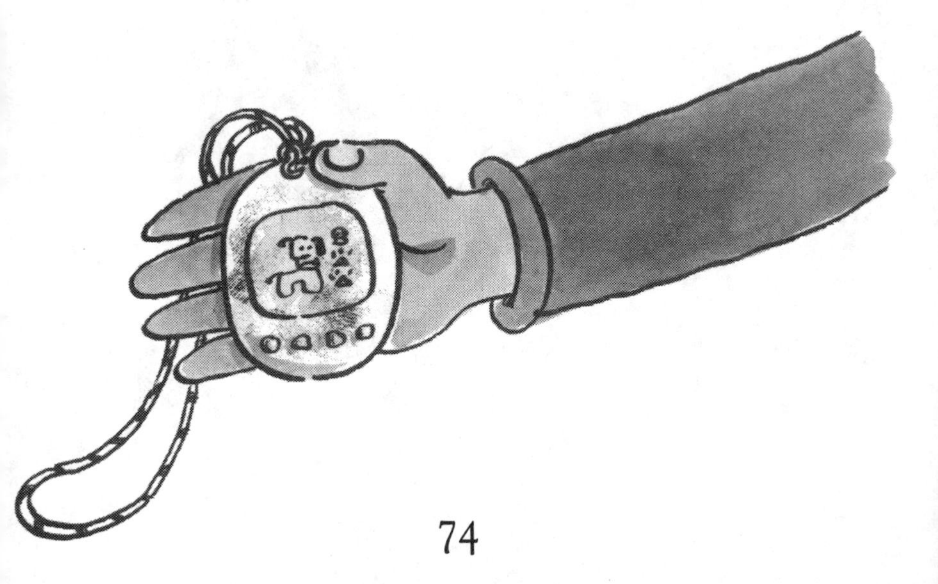

"Ruff! Ruff!" barked Trixie, dancing around excitedly.

"Sorry, Trixie, you can't have it back." Sam picked up the little dog. "But you're a smart girl to find it again, so I'm going to take you into the kitchen and give you some food that won't make you sick. You'll like that, won't you?"

"Ruff!" Trixie licked Sam's chin as she carried her off.

Jovan wiped the mud from Henry's screen. "He looks really sick," he said.

BE-EP, BE-EP, BE-EP, BE-EP! coughed the cyber pet.

"It *sounds* sick," said Katie. "Do you think you can cure it, Jo?"

"I don't know," he said sadly. "I'd better ask my dad to have a look."

"But Jo, your dad's a *vet*," said Matthew. "He cures animals, not electronic pets."

Jovan shrugged. "He fixed our video machine when it broke."

All the same, he didn't feel very hopeful as he made his way home. He kept thinking of Martin Bagshaw in the hospital, having his tonsils out. And—even worse—of Martin Bagshaw coming home from the hospital and expecting to find his cyber pet safe and well.

Instead, his cyber pet was probably even sicker than Martin.

Dr. Roy examined Henry on the kitchen table. Gravely he shook his head. "Looks pretty hopeless," he admitted. "What happened?"

Jovan told him about Trixie burying the cyber pet in the garden. Dr. Roy grinned. "Good old Trixie," he said. "Sounds like she's being allowed to behave like a real dog at last."

"It's not funny, Dad," said Jovan. "How am I going to explain it to Martin Bagshaw?"

But the worst was yet to come.

By Thursday morning the cyber pet had disappeared from the screen. In its place was an angel with a halo and twinkling stars.

Now Jovan had a real problem on his hands.

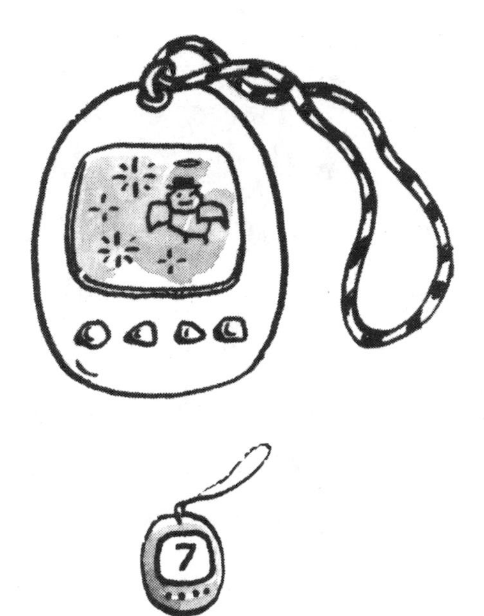

Good Luck!

As soon as Sam saw Jovan's gloomy face she guessed that the worst had happened. "Never mind, Jo," she said comfortingly. "You did your best."

Jovan slumped down on the couch. He took the dead cyber pet out of his pocket and stared at it glumly. "Martin comes out of the hospital today. He'll expect to find Henry waiting for him. I don't know what I'm going to say."

"Tell him the truth," said Sam. "After all, it was Trixie's fault, not yours. I'm sure he'll understand."

"I should never have left Henry alone with her." Jovan looked around the room. "Where is she?"

"Gone for a walk with Matthew and Katie."

"Did she eat that food I gave you yesterday?" asked Jovan.

"Yes, every bit! And it didn't make her sick either. She seems really strong this morning. Tons of energy."

"Looks like my dad was right, then," said Jovan. "All she needed was a sensible diet."

Sam nodded. "The trouble is, how are we going to persuade Mrs. Potter-Bunn to feed her properly from now on?"

Jovan sighed. "Pity she doesn't have a cyber pet instead," he said, staring down sadly at Henry. "She'd soon learn that if you don't give a dog healthy meals and plenty of discipline and games to play, it gets unhappy and sick."

At that moment Trixie shot into the room, followed by a hot-looking Matthew and Katie. "Whew!" said Matthew. "For a small dog she can run really fast! She saw a rabbit and wanted to chase it, but we couldn't keep up."

"She dragged us through a hedge," said Katie. "And nearly disappeared down a hole."

They both collapsed onto the couch. Trixie sat down, panting, her small pink tongue hanging out and her hair all over her face.

"Where's her ribbon?" asked Sam.

Matthew and Katie looked blank. "She must have lost it when she wriggled through the hedge," said Matthew.

Sam sighed. "I'd better find some string."

Jovan said, "My dad says this is probably the first time she's ever been allowed to behave like a real dog."

"She's a real dog all right!" said Matthew. "By the way, Jo, we just saw Martin Bagshaw. He asked where you were so we told him he'd find you here. He should be coming over any minute."

Jovan groaned.

"How's Henry?" asked Matthew.

"Died and gone to heaven," said Jovan sadly.

"Poor little cyber pet," said Katie.

The doorbell rang. Trixie started barking.

"That's Martin," said Jovan, getting to his feet. "I'll answer it."

He went into the hall. Seconds later he returned with Martin Bagshaw.

"Hello, Martin," said Sam. "How did you do in the hospital?"

"Great!" he said. "They gave me lots of ice cream. Where's Henry?"

Reluctantly Jovan gave the cyber pet back to Martin. "I'm afraid he got sick," he said. "I tried to save him, but it was too late. He died this morning."

"Oh," said Martin. He stared down at

Henry's face.

"We're all very sorry," said Sam. "But honestly, it wasn't Jo's fault. He did his best."

Martin shrugged. "It doesn't matter. They never live very long anyway. Henry was very old for a cyber pet." He started to press some buttons.

"What are you doing?" asked Katie, peering over his shoulder.

"Making a new one," said Martin. "This will be Henry IV."

Jovan stared at him. "You really don't mind?"

"I mind a *bit*," said Martin. "But not an *enormous* amount."

"But you seemed so miserable before you went into the hospital! I thought it was because you were worried about Henry?"

"I was a lot more worried about having my tonsils out. But you were right, it wasn't so bad and the nurses were nice." Martin stuffed Henry IV in his pocket and headed for the door. "Thanks, Jo."

Jovan saw him out. When he came back he said, "I wish I'd known before that he was only scared about having his tonsils out. I hardly slept at all last night because I was worrying about his cyber pet!"

On Friday afternoon, Sam packed Trixie's toys back in the suitcases. She brushed out the bed, took the food containers out of the refrigerator, and tied up Trixie's topknot with the neatest piece of string she could find.

At four o'clock the other Petsitters arrived. Even Dad came out of his den. They all sat in the living room and waited.

At last the doorbell rang. Trixie was the first to reach the hall. As soon as she saw Mrs. Potter-Bunn she leaped into her arms and started licking her face.

"Oh, my precious!" Tears came into Mrs. Potter-Bunn's eyes. "I've missed you so much. Have you missed me?"

"Ruff!" barked Trixie.

"Oh, you've lost your red bow! Never mind, I've brought you back some new ribbons—pale blue and lemon. They'll look beautiful on you."

Mr. Potter-Bunn snorted. He followed his wife into the living room, his mustache twitching like mad.

"Get her luggage, Gerald, and take it out to the car." Suddenly she spotted the still-full food containers. "Oh dear, wouldn't she eat? I did warn you she has a delicate stomach."

"We-ell," said Sam, trying hard to be tactful. "The food you left seemed to make her sick, so we. . . ."

"Ah, yes. She's often sick, I'm afraid. Did she eat anything?"

"Actually she's eaten quite a bit," said Sam. "Dr. Roy, the vet, gave us some special dog food for her. It didn't make her sick at all. In fact, she seemed to like it."

Mrs. Potter-Bunn looked amazed. She turned to her husband. "Did you hear that, Gerald? Special dog food."

"I heard," growled Mr. Potter-Bunn. "It's what I've been telling you for ages."

"We took her for a walk," said Matthew. "And she really enjoyed it."

Mrs. Potter-Bunn looked even more amazed. "Did you hear that, Gerald? They took her for a walk!"

"I heard," growled Mr. Potter-Bunn. "She enjoyed it, I bet."

Mrs. Potter-Bunn stared at the happy, healthy little dog in her arms. "She certainly looks very well. Maybe I should try giving her some of Dr. Roy's special dog food in the future. Did you have any left?"

"Yes, I'll get it for you." Sam went to the kitchen and came back with the bag.

"Thank you," said Mrs. Potter-Bunn, still looking slightly stunned. "Take these out to the car, Gerald. Oh, and bring in the gift we brought back for these smart boys and girls."

The gift turned out to be the most enormous box of chocolates Sam had ever seen. "They look delicious. Thank you very much," said Sam. "And could you please sign our community service form?"

Matthew took out the form. Mrs. Potter-Bunn signed it with a flourish.

"You've done very well," said Mrs. Potter-Bunn with a gracious nod of her head. "I will recommend your petsitting service to all my friends."

She followed her husband down the walk with Trixie draped over her shoulder. The Petsitters crowded onto the doorstep to wave.

"Goodbye, Trixie!" Katie called.

"Good rabbit-chasing!" called Matthew.

"Good digging!" called Jovan.

"Good luck!" called Sam.

"Ruff!" barked Trixie.

And Sam was almost sure she winked at them.

The End

The Petsitters Club

Keeps Kids Laughing!

Sam, Jo, Matthew, and Katie are four animal-loving kids who run a pet-sitting service. They mind pets for busy animal owners—everything from puppies and kittens to exotic creatures like donkeys, snakes, and lizards. The kids are funny, imaginative, and energetic—but more often than not, they run into trouble. Kids who haven't read all Petsitters Club books will want to select from this complete titles list.

by Tessa Krailing,
Illustrations by Jan Lewis
Each book: paperback, 96 pp.,
$3.95, Canada $4.95 Available at most bookstores

Vol.1: Jilly the Kid
ISBN 0-7641-0569-8

Vol.2: The Cat Burglar
ISBN 0-7641-0570-1

Vol.3: Donkey Rescue
ISBN 0-7641-0572-8

Vol.4: Snake Alarm
ISBN 0-7641-0573-6

Vol.5: Scruncher Goes Wandering
ISBN 0-7641-0574-4

Vol.6: Trixie and the Cyber Pet
ISBN 0-7641-0614-7

Vol.7: Oscar the Fancy Rat
ISBN 0-7641-0692-9

Vol.8: Where's Iggy?
ISBN 0-7641-0693-7

Vol.9: Pony Trouble
ISBN 0-7641-0736-4

Vol.10: The Rude Parrot
ISBN 0-7641-1193-0

Vacation Special: Monkey Puzzle
ISBN 0-7641-0737-2

Winter Special: The Christmas Kitten
ISBN 0-7641-1184-1

Barron's Educational Series, Inc. • 250 Wireless Blvd., Hauppauge, NY 11788
In Canada: Georgetown Book Warehouse, 34 Armstrong Ave., Georgetown, Ont. L7G 4R9
Visit our Web Site @ www.barronseduc.com

Join The Petsitters Club for *more* animal adventures!

1. Jilly the Kid
2. The Cat Burglar
3. Donkey Rescue
4. Snake Alarm!
5. Scruncher Goes Wandering